Josephine Wants To Dance

Written by Jackie French

Illustrated by Bruce Whatley

Angus&Robertson
An imprint of HarperCollins*Publishers*

Angus&Robertson
An imprint of HarperCollins*Publishers*, Australia

First published in Australia in 2006
by HarperCollins*Publishers* Australia Pty Limited
ABN 36 009 913 517
www.harpercollins.com.au

Text copyright © Jackie French 2006
Illustrations copyright © Farmhouse Illustration Company Pty Limited 2006

HarperCollins*Publishers*
Level 13, 201 Elizabeth Street, Sydney, NSW 2000, Australia
31 View Road, Glenfield, Auckland 10, New Zealand
77–85 Fulham Palace Road, London W6 8JB, United Kingdom
2 Bloor Street East, 20th Floor, Toronto, Ontario M4W 1AA, Canada
10 East 53rd Street, New York NY 10032, USA

National Library of Australia Cataloguing-in-Publication data:

French, Jackie.
    Josephine wants to dance.
    1st ed.
    For primary school children.
    ISBN 978 0 20720 075 5.
    ISBN 0 207 20075 0.
    I. Whatley, Bruce. II. Title.
A823.3

    Paperback edition
    ISBN 978 0 20720 080 9.
    ISBN 0 207 20080 7.

Bruce Whatley used acrylic paints on watercolour paper to create the illustrations for this book
Cover and internal design by Natalie Winter
Colour reproduction by Graphic Print Group, Adelaide, South Australia
Printed in China by RR Donnelley on 128gsm Matt Art

7 6 5   13 14 15

To Fuchsia, the roo who danced around our lives,
and to Bruce, who turns words into magic. JF

To my new friend Phoebe R, who loves to line dance. BW

Josephine loved to dance.

She bounced with the brolgas ...

and leapt with the lyrebirds.

'Kangaroos don't dance,
Josephine!'
said her little brother Joey.
'They hop.'

But Josephine took no notice.

The emus showed her how to point her toes.
The eagles taught her how to soar
to the music of the wind.

Josephine whirled like the clouds across the gully.
She swayed with the branches in the trees.

But still she dreamt of
somehow finding another
way to dance.

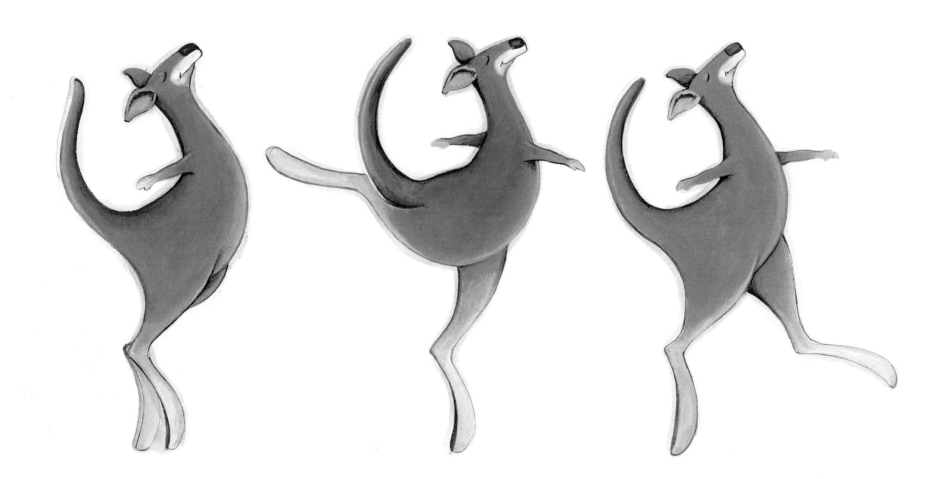

'There has to be something **more**!' said Josephine wistfully as she danced across her brother.

'Kangaroos don't dance, Josephine!' yelled Joey, ducking his head. 'They jump.'

But Josephine kept on dancing.

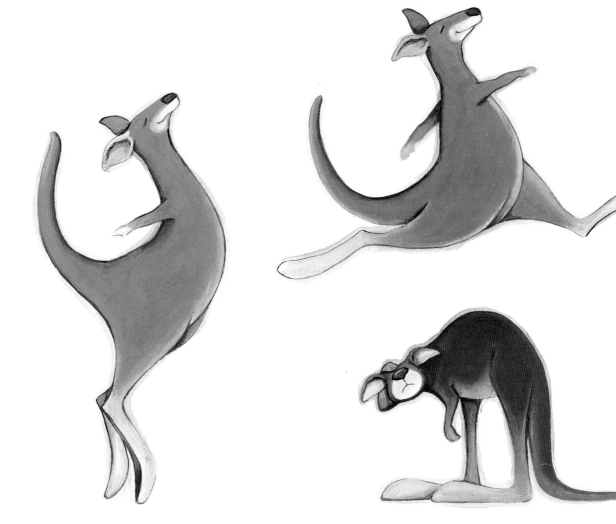
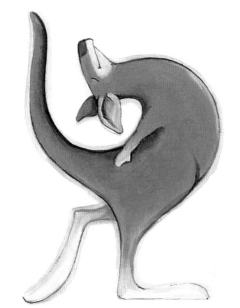

The next day Josephine found
posters stuck on the trees. The ballet
was coming to Shaggy Gully!

'That's how I'd like to dance!'
cried Josephine. 'In a pink tutu,
with silk ballet shoes.'

'Get real!' said Joey.
'Kangaroos don't wear tutus, Josephine!
And they never wear silk ballet shoes.'

'I'm going to,' said Josephine,
pointing her toes.

She crept over to the hall …

and peered through
the window as the
dancers rehearsed.

A week later Josephine
sneaked into town.

'Ohhh!' cried Josephine.

She watched the dancers for hours.
Then she practised at night … all alone.

She spun, she swirled, she pirouetted …
and at the end she always curtsied.

'I really am becoming a dancer now,'
thought Josephine.

The day of the first
performance arrived.
But the ballet company
was in trouble!

'Ow!' shrieked the prima ballerina as she twisted her ankle.

'Ohhh!' sobbed the understudy as she found a splinter in her toe.

'Who will dance the lead role?'
cried the ballet director.

'Who else can leap so high?'

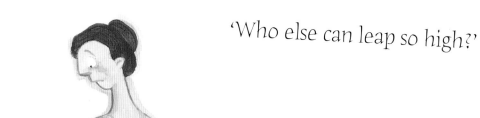

Josephine jumped ...

through the window ...
    and onto the stage.

'A kangaroo!' yelled the dancers.

'There's a kangaroo on the stage!'

Josephine pointed her toes. She tossed her head.

She swayed like the lyrebirds as they call to their sweethearts.

She soared like an eagle through the sky.

'A dancing kangaroo!' everyone cried.
'Who ever heard of a dancing kangaroo?'

Josephine swirled above the stage like the mist playing with the moon.

The director stared at Josephine.
Finally, she smiled. 'Well, this kangaroo
can dance – and she knows the lead role.
And she can jump higher than
any other dancer I've seen!'

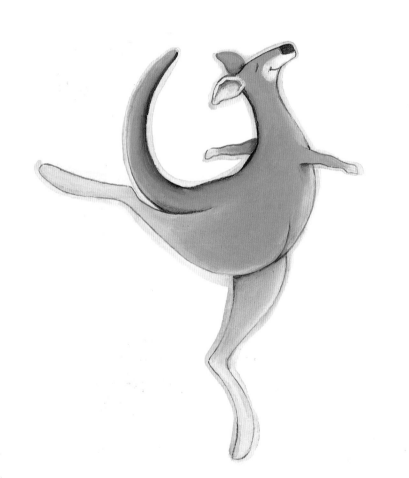

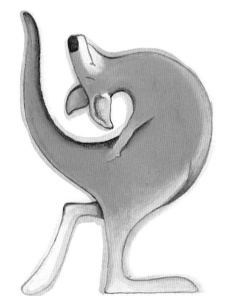

The director took Josephine
to the wardrobe department.

'A kangaroo!' exclaimed the costume designer.

'I can't dress a kangaroo!'

'Just do your best,'
the director told him.

The costume designer quickly altered a tutu for Josephine.

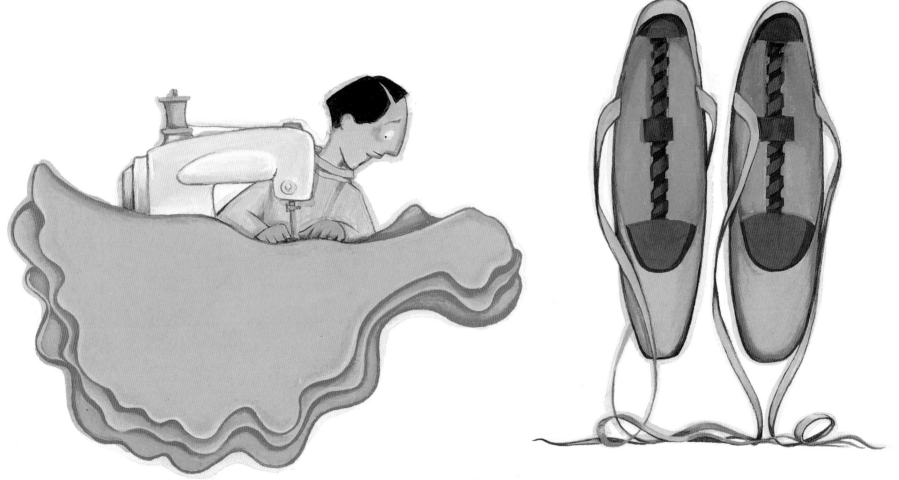

He stretched some ballet shoes too. They were probably the longest ballet shoes in the world.

At last it was time
for the performance.
The audience took their seats.
The orchestra tuned up.

Josephine stood backstage,
waiting for the music to begin.

'Josephine!' hissed Joey
through the window.
'What are you doing?
Come back to the bush
at once!'

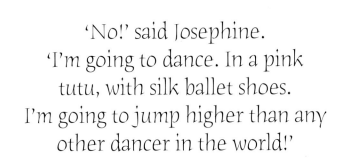

'No!' said Josephine.
'I'm going to dance. In a pink
tutu, with silk ballet shoes.
I'm going to jump higher than any
other dancer in the world!'

The lights dimmed.
The orchestra started playing.
The curtains opened.
The performance began.

The ballerinas fluttered onto the stage …   one …   two …   three …

four ...   and ...   Josephine!

Someone in the audience giggled. 'It's a kangaroo!'

Then Josephine began to dance.

She twirled through the air like leaves in a whirlwind.
She leapt like no dancer ever had before.
And at the end she curtsied like the brolgas bowing to the sun.

The audience were silent.

And then they clapped.

And then they ... cheered!

'This kangaroo is a dancer!' they cried.

'A truly magnificent dancer!'

Josephine was still curtsying
when the ballet director brought
bunches of roses onto the stage.

'Roses are delicious!' decided Josephine.

'And I am finally a dancer – and it's fun!'

In fact, dancing
looked like so much
fun that soon all
the audience ...

were bounding and bouncing ... and prancing and pouncing ... bumping and jumping ...

and leaping and thumping …

swishing and swirling …

and twinkle-toe twirling …

but nobody **ever** danced quite like ...

Josephine!